Figaro

Excitable and ready for adventure, Figaro knows
the neighbourhood like the back of his paw.

Pixie

Pixie has a nose for trouble
and a very active imagination!

Katsumi

Sleek and sophisticated,
Katsumi is quick to call Kitty
at the first sign of trouble.

OXFORD
UNIVERSITY PRESS

Great Clarendon Street, Oxford OX2 6DP
Oxford University Press is a department of the University of Oxford.
It furthers the University's objective of excellence in research, scholarship,
and education by publishing worldwide. Oxford is a registered trade mark
of Oxford University Press in the UK and in certain other countries

British Library Cataloguing in Publication Data

Data available

ISBN: 978-0-19-278415-5

1 3 5 7 9 10 8 6 4 2

Printed in Great Britain by Bell and Bain Ltd, Glasgow

Paper used in the production of this book is a natural,
recyclable product made from wood grown in sustainable forests.
The manufacturing process conforms to the environmental
regulations of the country of origin.

Here's to you, Jenny—pencil wizard
extraordinaire! - P.H.

To Lizzie, Gillian, Rob and
everyone on Team Kitty! - J.L.

Kitty

and the
Runaway Train

OXFORD
UNIVERSITY PRESS

Chapter 1

'Wow, look at all the decorations!'
Kitty gazed around the train station.

There were silver and red
streamers strung from every pillar along
with bunches of balloons. A banner
hanging on the station wall read:

TAKE A RIDE ON THE RED ROCKET!

Kitty had come to the train station with her mum, dad, and little brother Max, to see the Red Rocket. The famous steam train would be arriving at six o'clock that evening on its record-breaking journey to visit every station in the whole country in ten days.

Kitty looked at the station clock— it was five minutes to six. She held her dad's hand tightly and stood on tiptoes to peep through the crowd.

She had never seen the place so
busy. She wished she could clamber
up a pillar to watch the train arriving,

4

but she knew she couldn't use her
superpowers with so many people
around.

Kitty had an awesome secret—she had cat-like superpowers just like her mum. Her special powers meant she could climb, jump, and balance with amazing skill. She often went out on missions with her cat crew, running across the rooftops in the moonlight and helping creatures in trouble.

Her superpowered senses let her see in the dark and hear things from miles away. Most exciting of all, Kitty had the power to talk to animals and her best friend was a little ginger kitten called Pumpkin.

'Where's the train, Daddy?' Max tugged at their dad's hand. 'I can't see!'

'It'll be here soon.' Dad lifted Max onto his shoulders so he could get a better view.

Kitty focused on using her superpowered senses. With her cat-like hearing, she caught a distant chugging sound. Then she spotted a puff of steam rising into the air. 'Look, there it is! The train's coming.'

With a cheery choo-woo the Red Rocket zoomed round the corner and then slowed down as it drew into the station. Its engine gleamed in the evening light. The crowd clapped and cheered, and the train driver leant out of the window to wave at everyone.

'Daddy, look! There's the driver,' cried Max, excitedly.

'I wish we could have a ride,' said Kitty. 'It looks amazing!'

'The train won't set off again till tomorrow morning,' explained Mum.

'Lots of very important people will be on board to travel to the very last station. The train has to be there by eleven o'clock to break the world record!'

The train came to a stop and the passengers began to pour out of the carriages with their bags. Kitty spotted a little black cat jumping down from the train, but lost sight of her in the crowd.

Once the platform cleared, Dad took Max and Kitty to have a closer look at the train. Kitty touched the shiny paintwork and gazed at the huge wheels.

'I'm afraid we have to go,' Dad said at last. 'It's nearly your bedtime, Max.'

'I don't want to go! I want the train.' Max's cheeks grew red and his eyes filled with tears.

'Why don't I read you your *Millie the Magic Train* book before you go to bed?' Kitty said to her little brother. 'And I promise to play trains with you tomorrow.'

Max nodded and stuck his thumb in his mouth. Dad lifted Max onto his shoulders again and they headed out of the station.

Kitty turned to take one last look at the Red Rocket. The polished paintwork gleamed in the light of the setting sun. Kitty noticed two cats walking down the platform and checking inside each carriage. A large cat with smoky-grey fur led the way while a scruffy-looking cat with sandy fur trailed after him.

The cats glanced at Kitty and the grey one raised a paw to say hello. Kitty smiled and waved back, before hurrying after her mum and dad. Did the cats live at the station, she wondered? She'd never heard of train cats, but maybe Pumpkin would know.

* * *

'Oh, yes! There are two station cats,' Pumpkin said when Kitty asked him about the cats later that evening. 'The grey one, Skipper, has lived there

14

for years and Yuma is his assistant. They keep an eye on the station and take care of animal passengers.'

Kitty and Pumpkin were sitting on Kitty's window seat watching the moon rising over the rooftops.

Max had gone to sleep after Kitty read him a story and Mum had hurried out to do her superhero work. Street lamps lit up the roads far below and tiny stars were gleaming in the night sky.

'I wish you'd seen the train, Pumpkin.' Kitty stroked Pumpkin's ginger ears. 'The engine was enormous. I didn't go inside but Mum said the carriages are beautiful with polished tables and velvet seats, and they have a restaurant carriage where they cook you anything you want, and you eat it off silver plates.'

Pumpkin yawned and stretched. 'Ooh, that sounds fancy! I'd love to go and see it, but I'm soooo sleepy.'

Kitty smiled. 'Well, it is quite late. Maybe we should get ready for bed.' She was about to climb down from the window seat, when there was a soft tapping at the window.

Kitty opened the window to find Figaro outside. Beside him was a little black cat with a white-tipped tail that looked just like him. Kitty recognized her as the kitten she'd spotted getting off the train earlier that day.

'Hello, Figaro!' Kitty said in surprise. 'Are you all right?'

'I wish I was, Kitty!' sighed Figaro, clutching his cheek with one paw. 'This is a COMPLETE disaster!'

'Come in!' Kitty helped Figaro and the smaller cat inside.

'This is my niece, Minette,' Figaro explained. 'She arrived on the Red Rocket this evening to visit me.'

'Hi, Minette,' said Kitty. 'Did you enjoy your ride on the steam train?'

'Yes, I liked the train, but then I lost my Fluff!' Minette's whiskers trembled.

'She lost her stuffed panda, Fluff,' Figaro explained. 'She takes him everywhere and she misses him terribly. We've looked all over the city, but we can't find him anywhere.'

'I can't sleep without my Fluff!' mewed Minette.

Figaro flopped onto Kitty's bed

and sighed dramatically. 'I'm so tired I can't move another step! Please could you help us, Kitty? It's cold and dark out there and it looks like it might rain.'

Kitty peered out into the darkness. The wind blew strongly, rocking the trees and sending leaves skittering across the pavement. Minette wiped a tear off her furry cheek.

'We can help find Fluff, can't we?' Pumpkin asked Kitty.

'Yes, I'm sure we can!' Kitty crouched beside Minette. 'Do you have any idea where you left the panda? Did you pick him up when you got off the train?'

Minette's face crumpled. 'I don't know!'

'I forgot to check the train,' said Figaro. 'Yes, I bet that's where he is.'

Kitty quickly pulled on her superhero outfit and mask. 'We'll look there first. You two should stay here and get some rest. I'm sure we won't be long.'

'Thank you, Kitty!' Figaro patted

the tearful Minette, before stretching out on the bed.

Kitty climbed onto the windowsill. 'Are you sure you want to come?' she asked Pumpkin. 'You could stay here in the warm with Figaro if you wanted.'

Pumpkin skipped after Kitty. 'I
want to see the famous train with the
enormous engine. I'm wide awake now
and ready for an adventure!'

23

Chapter 2

Kitty felt her superpowers tingling inside her as she stepped out into the bright moonlight. She and Pumpkin skipped across the rooftops together, giggling. Kitty tried out some of the new moves that she'd been practising

in her bedroom, cartwheeling along
the top of the roof and doing a double
somersault over a chimney pot.

'That was amazing!' squeaked
Pumpkin.

'Thanks!' Kitty lifted the kitten
onto her shoulder and jumped from
one roof to the next, her cape flying out
behind her.

At last, they saw the station in the
distance with the railway line beyond it.
Kitty hurried across the rooftops. Then
she leapt onto the station roof and slid

down one of the pillars onto
the platform.

The Red Rocket stood
silently, the moonlight
glistening on its shiny
carriages. Kitty remembered
the noise of the engine and
how steam had gushed out
of its chimney. It was
strange to see the train so
quiet and still.

'Look at that! It really
is gigantic.' Pumpkin eyed the

train in wonder.

Two cats peered down at them from the roof of the train. Kitty recognized them as the station cats she'd spotted earlier that evening.

The cat with smoky-grey fur leapt down from the train roof. 'It's all right, Yuma!' he called back. 'It's the superhero girl I was telling you about.'

Kitty smiled shyly. She wasn't used to hearing herself called a superhero girl. 'Hello! I'm Kitty and this is Pumpkin.'

'Nice to meet you at last, Kitty. My friend, Cleo from the museum, has told me all about you,' said the grey cat. 'I'm Skipper and this is my trainee, Yuma.'

'Sorry to wake you up,' said Kitty. 'A friend of ours thinks she left something on the train, so we came to look.'

'Oh, we weren't asleep,' Skipper purred. 'We were polishing the train roof. The Red Rocket must look her best for tomorrow.'

'She's going to look smashing!' Yuma said, leaping down from the train roof to join them.

'So, you said your friend had lost something?' asked Skipper. 'I'll see if it's in my Lost Property Log. Come this way!' He herded them all into the Station Office.

Kitty explained about Fluff, the stuffed panda, and how Minette might have left her toy on the train.

Skipper flicked through the Lost Property Log with one paw. 'Well, it isn't in my log. Yuma, did you check the train thoroughly after the passengers got off?'

Yuma nodded. 'Oh, yes! I found three hats, two phones, and a toothbrush, but no pandas.'

'Are you sure you looked everywhere?' asked Skipper. 'It's a big train, you know.'

'Yes, Skipper, but I'm happy to search all the carriages again.' Yuma dashed to the door.

'No, you'd better wait here. I don't want anyone on the Red Rocket without me,' said Skipper with a frown.

'Please let me look!' cried Yuma. 'If I'm training to be a station cat, I need to prove that I can be useful.'

Skipper sighed. 'All right then. But don't get paw smudges everywhere!'

'Can I come too?' cried Pumpkin. 'I want to see the velvet seats and the restaurant with the silver plates.'

'I'll show you around!' Yuma said eagerly. 'There's an ice-cream machine in the restaurant too. Come and see!'

The two cats hurried out of the Station Office. Kitty tugged impatiently at her superhero mask. She wanted to see inside the train too, but she didn't want to be rude and run away while

Skipper was talking.

'It's a good life being a station cat,' Skipper told her. 'But there's a lot of responsibility. Sometimes passengers get lost, or they get on the wrong train, and there's always so much lost property. Once, someone even left a whole birthday cake behind!'

'Oh dear, I hope they found it again.'

Kitty watched Yuma and Pumpkin cross the platform. They scampered up the train steps and disappeared inside the carriage.

'Oh, yes, they came back to get it—thank goodness.' Skipper frowned and flicked through the Lost Property Log again.

'Maybe we should help the others check the train?' Kitty suggested.

'Let me look through this log one more time.' Skipper stroked his grey whiskers. 'Hmm, now what were we looking for? A panda?'

The lights went on inside the Red Rocket and Kitty heard Pumpkin and Yuma giggling inside.

She couldn't wait any longer. 'I'll just pop out and see if they're all right.'

But as she headed out of the Station Office the train whistle suddenly went choo-woo! Then the engine started to rumble. Kitty stopped in surprise. Why was the whistle sounding? The train wasn't leaving till the next morning.

The sound of the engine grew
louder. Then a great gush of steam rose
from the train chimney.

Skipper bounded out of the office.
'What's going on? No one is allowed to
touch that engine.'

'Pumpkin!' called Kitty. 'Are you all right?'

Pumpkin's face appeared at the carriage window. His whiskers were shaking, and his eyes were wide with fright. 'Help, help! It's an emergency.'

The Red Rocket began to chug

forwards—slowly at first—then faster and faster. Kitty hurried down the platform towards Pumpkin.

'Someone's stealing the train!' yelled Skipper. 'Robbers! Bandits! Thieves!'

Kitty's heart pounded. Who could be stealing the Red Rocket?

'Kitty, help!' Pumpkin called again. 'I don't know what to do.'

Kitty started running alongside the train. 'Just stay there, Pumpkin!' she shouted. 'I'll come and get you.'

Another puff of steam poured
out of the chimney. The pistons moved
round and round and the train began to

gain speed. Pumpkin's little face stared
back at Kitty as the Red Rocket began
rushing away into the dark.

Chapter 3

Kitty raced down the platform like lightning. The Red Rocket was getting faster and faster. She had to reach Pumpkin before it pulled away from the station. She pumped her arms

and legs as fast as she could.
Her superpowers tingled through her
body.

Skipper was running at her heels.
'We-have-to-catch-up!' he puffed.

Kitty looked around quickly. She
was sure she'd catch the train more
easily if she ran along the rooftops.

She shinned up a pillar onto the station roof and Skipper climbed after her.

'I'm going to leap onto the roof of the train!' she yelled back. 'It's the only way to reach the engine.'

'I'm right beside you, Kitty!' puffed Skipper.

Kitty raced across the station roof and leapt from one rooftop to the next, the train chugging along below her. The railway tracks stretched into the distance, glittering in the moonlight.

Kitty glanced down at the train. She was used to balancing on rooftops, but she'd never leapt onto a moving train before! Railway tracks were dangerous places that ordinary people had to keep away from. Kitty knew she could never have tried rescuing Pumpkin if she didn't have superpowers.

She would have to time her jump exactly right. If she was too slow, the train would run away down the track.

If she jumped too soon, she could lose her balance and tumble off the roof. Her stomach flipped over. What if her superpowers weren't strong enough?

Then she caught sight of

Pumpkin's scared face at the carriage window. She'd promised him she was coming to get him and that was exactly what she was going to do. She tried to remember what her mum had said before her very first superhero

adventure. *Don't let fear hold you back.*
You're braver than you think!

She would be brave for Pumpkin.
She sprinted even faster, ready to take
the leap.

'No, Kitty—wait!' called Skipper.
'There's a fence up ahead.'

The train rushed towards a metal
footbridge. Kitty sprang onto the
bottom step just as the Red Rocket
raced under the bridge and away round
a corner. A tall fence marked No Entry
blocked their way. Kitty knew by the

time she'd climbed it the train would
be gone.

'What are we going to do now?'
cried Skipper. 'Lots of very important
people are supposed to be riding on the
Red Rocket tomorrow morning. What
will they say if the train's gone missing?'

Kitty climbed back to the rooftops
and gazed at the disappearing train. She
pictured Pumpkin clinging to a seat as
the Red Rocket carried him far away.
Poor Pumpkin! They had been best
friends for a long time and Kitty knew

how easily he got scared. Yuma would be frightened too.

Skipper groaned. 'We've got to catch that train robber! Yuma won't know what to do. He's new to the job. I never should have let him onto the train by himself. This is all my fault!'

'It isn't your fault at all!' said Kitty.
'None of us knew the train would be
stolen.'

Skipper prowled up and down,
shaking his whiskers worriedly. 'I really
wanted everything to be perfect for the

Red Rocket's final journey tomorrow.'

'Do you have any idea who could have done this?' asked Kitty.

'It seems like the work of a robber dog,' Skipper growled. 'Maybe a Marauding Mastiff or a Beagle Bandit!'

'There MUST be a way to catch up with them.' Kitty gazed at the rows of street lamps criss-crossing the city. She could just make out the train hurtling down the railway track in the distance. Suddenly, she had an idea.

'I know! The railway track goes

under another bridge not far from my house. We can take a shortcut and wait for the train there.'

'Good thinking, Kitty!' said Skipper. 'Why don't you lead the way?'

Kitty dashed across the rooftops, heading towards home. The wind grew stronger, and rain began to fall. The rooftops became slippery, and Kitty worked hard to keep her balance. She and Skipper hurried across the rooftops and climbed onto a footbridge with crisscross railings spanning the train track.

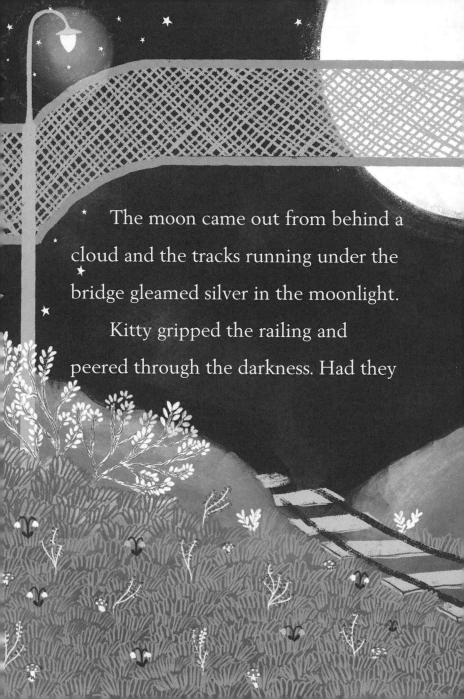

The moon came out from behind a cloud and the tracks running under the bridge gleamed silver in the moonlight. Kitty gripped the railing and peered through the darkness. Had they

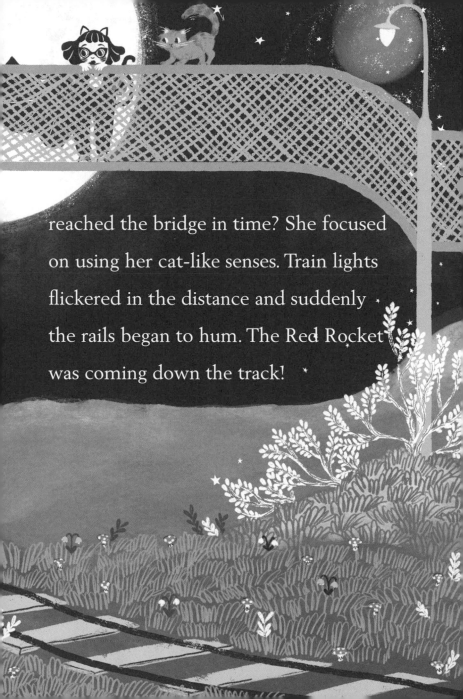

reached the bridge in time? She focused
on using her cat-like senses. Train lights
flickered in the distance and suddenly
the rails began to hum. The Red Rocket
was coming down the track!

'We have to be ready to jump!'
Kitty told Skipper. 'I'll go first. Then
you can follow me.'

The Red Rocket raced around the
corner. The pistons swung like huge
metal arms and great puffs of steam
rose from the chimney.

Kitty balanced on the bridge with
her black cape swirling around her. Her
superpowers buzzed inside her like
electricity. 'Are you ready?' she called
to Skipper.

Skipper waved his paws wildly.
'No, no! This isn't going to work.'

'It's OK—I can do this!' said Kitty.
'You wait here, and I'll stop the train.'

'I've just remembered!' Skipper
shouted over the roar of the train.

'The Red Rocket's on the wrong track. If it stays on this line it'll come to a dead end and roll down the hill into a ditch. Don't worry—I can switch the tracks before it's too late!' He rushed away from the bridge, following the railway line.

Kitty fixed her eyes on the Red Rocket. The train was only seconds away. She had to get this jump just right. Then she could get inside the carriage to rescue Pumpkin and Yuma.

The Red Rocket zoomed down the track towards her.

Kitty clutched the bridge tightly and held her breath. Just as the train sped under the bridge, she leapt into the dark. The wind rushed past her. She somersaulted through the air and landed gracefully on the train roof.

Choo-woo! The Red Rocket let out another puff of steam.

Kitty crouched on top of the train, steadying herself with one hand. Her heart pounded. The train rattled and wobbled beneath her, but she kept her balance. She'd done it! All she had to do now was get inside to find Yuma and Pumpkin.

What would Figaro say if he could see her now? He'd be amazed that the search for the toy panda had led to a wild ride on the roof of the Red Rocket!

Chapter

4

The train hurtled down the
railway track with Kitty crouching on
the roof. She could see Skipper racing
up the grassy bank towards a tall grey
box with three levers sticking out of
the top. The station cat leapt on to the

box and pulled the right-hand lever, but nothing happened.

Kitty watched nervously as the train rushed along. Would Skipper manage to switch the tracks in time?

Skipper tugged the lever again. There was a screeching sound. Then the Red Rocket swerved onto the next track.

'Well done, Skipper!' Kitty shouted.

'Watch out, Kitty!' Skipper yelled back. 'There's a tun—'

The wind roared in Kitty's ears,

and she missed what Skipper was saying. She used her superpowered balance and crept carefully along the roof. If she could reach the end of the carriage, she could swing down from the roof and climb inside.

The wind grew stronger, and rain began to fall again. Kitty stumbled on the slippery train roof. Gasping, she grabbed the edge of the roof with her fingertips. Then she wiped the raindrops from her eyes and inched forwards a little more.

Suddenly a black shape loomed out of the shadows.

A tunnel!

Kitty's heart pounded. That must have been what Skipper was trying to tell her. The Red Rocket was hurtling towards a tunnel. If she didn't get inside quickly it would be too late!

The train rattled below her. The pitch-black tunnel grew closer and closer.

Kitty dashed towards the end

of the carriage. Skidding on the wet roof, she swung over the side between the two carriages. A small ladder led downwards. Kitty dropped onto the step at the bottom and fumbled with the door handle. The door swung inwards, and she jumped inside just as the train zoomed into the tunnel.

The twinkling streetlights disappeared as the train rushed deeper into the darkness. Kitty stared around the dimly lit carriage. It was just as beautiful as her mum had told her.

Red velvet seats lined the carriage and
paintings of flowers were pinned to the
walls.

Kitty crossed to the next carriage, but there was no sign of Pumpkin or Yuma. Hurrying through the next door, she found herself in the restaurant carriage. Neat menu cards written in gold letters stood on each of the tables. A huge silver ice-cream machine with twenty different flavours from pistachio to mango stood in the middle. There was a smudged paw mark on the button marked chocolate that looked exactly the size of Pumpkin's paw.

'Pumpkin, where are you?' Kitty cried.

She used her superpowered hearing and detected voices coming from the engine room at the front of the train. She ran to the next carriage and called again. 'Pumpkin? Yuma?'

'Kitty? Is that you?' Pumpkin called back.

'Help!' cried Yuma.

Kitty swallowed. Maybe the train robber had trapped the little cats. She wouldn't let them get away with it!

Kitty raced towards the front of the train. A shiver ran down her neck when

she reached the engine room.
Taking a deep breath, she tugged at
the door handle, and it swung open.

　　She stared around, her heart
thumping. Where was the train robber?

The engine room was a mass of bronze-coloured pipes alongside white dials and levers. Coal burned brightly in the chute at the bottom. The driver's seat was empty, but two scared-looking cats were huddled together behind it.

Pumpkin leapt up, his whiskers quivering. 'Kitty, you're here at last! We're really sorry! We never meant any of this to happen.'

'It was all just an accident,' said Yuma.

Kitty stared back at them. Then suddenly she understood what they meant. 'So, there isn't a train robber after all? You were the ones that started the train?'

'We didn't mean to,' gasped Yuma, 'I really hope Skipper believes me.'

'You can stop it, can't you Kitty? We tried but we couldn't move that lever.' Pumpkin's eyes were wide with fright.

'I hope so!' Kitty stepped up to

the control panel and grabbed the red lever marked Stop.

The Red Rocket chugged faster and faster. Trees and bridges rushed past the window. The engine groaned as if it was starting to overheat.

Kitty pulled the Stop lever as hard as she could, but it barely moved.

'There's a sharp bend coming!' cried Yuma. 'We're going too fast!'

'Hurry, Kitty!' gasped Pumpkin.

Kitty took a deep breath and

yanked the lever again. This time it moved.

The brakes screeched and the wheels began to slow. The chugging sound of the engine died away and at last the train juddered to a stop.

'You did it!' cried Yuma, leaping up and down.

'Thank you, Kitty. I was so scared.' Pumpkin jumped into Kitty's arms for a cuddle.

Kitty stroked his ears. 'You poor thing! But tell me what happened. How did you start the train in the first place?'

Yuma and Pumpkin exchanged
guilty looks.

'We didn't mean to be naughty,'
explained Pumpkin. 'It was just so
exciting being here in the engine room.
All the buttons looked so important
and shiny.'

'And I wanted to show Pumpkin
how everything works,' added Yuma.
'Skipper's told me what most of the
controls do.'

'So, we started playing trains,'

said Pumpkin. 'And Yuma was the driver, and I was his assistant. It was a lot of fun . . . until I accidentally pressed a button and the coals began to burn. Then every button we pressed seemed to make things worse.'

'We tried and tried to stop the train, but we couldn't! Do you think Skipper will be very cross with me?' Yuma flicked his tail worriedly.

Kitty thought of how hard Skipper had worked to switch the Red Rocket onto the right train track. 'We

ought to go back and find him. He had
to stop to switch the tracks and that
was a long way back before the tunnel.'

Suddenly, there was a tapping
at the window. A large tawny owl
perched on the windowsill, peering in
at them with bright orange eyes.

Kitty opened the window, and the owl flew inside.

'Hello, I'm Copperwing,' hooted the owl. 'I'm afraid I have some bad news.'

'Oh dear, what's wrong?' asked Kitty.

'There's an injured cat limping up the railway track,' explained Copperwing. 'I live in a tree close to the line and I spotted him while I was looking for food.'

'Oh, no, that could be Skipper!' said Kitty.

'He wanted me to look for a runaway train to find out if it had come to a stop,' added the owl. 'He said he didn't need any help but he was walking on three paws as if the other one was very sore.'

'Skipper never wants any help,' said Yuma, sadly. 'I'm supposed to be learning to be a station cat, but he hardly lets me do anything at all. Now that I've made such a big mistake, I bet he'll be even worse.'

'Thank you for telling us,' Kitty
said to the owl. 'We'll go back and
find him.'

'Good luck!' the owl hooted,

before flying off into the darkness.

'Quick, how do we change the direction of the train?' asked Kitty.

'Ignite the coals like this. Then pull this lever to send the train into reverse.' Yuma pointed to a green lever.

Kitty pulled the lever to make the Red Rocket go backwards. 'I hope we can find Skipper soon. If he's limping around on three legs, he really does need help this time.'

Chapter 5

The Red Rocket chugged back up the railway line and into the tunnel again. Kitty kept a careful eye on the engine's speed. If they went too fast, they would never find Skipper. Pumpkin and Yuma went to fetch the

train's first-aid kit just in case it was
needed.

The train drew out of the tunnel,
and they passed the place where
Skipper had switched the tracks. Kitty
stopped the train and climbed down
from the engine cab.

'Can you see Skipper?' Yuma
asked eagerly.

Kitty used her superpowered
vision to search the darkness. She
spotted moths fluttering in the night
sky and a mouse scurrying around a

bush, but she couldn't see Skipper.

'He can't have got very far if he
was limping on three legs,' she said
to the others. 'We just have to keep
looking.'

'Maybe he stopped for a nap,' suggested Pumpkin, with a yawn.

Kitty shook her head. 'He wanted everything to be perfect for the Red Rocket's final journey tomorrow.

I don't think he'll go to sleep till the train is safe and sound in the station again.'

'Skipper, where are you?' called Yuma, but there was no answer.

Kitty's skin tingled. She couldn't help feeling that something was wrong. She tried using her super hearing. Beneath the rustling of the trees, there was the sound of shuffling paw steps.

'This way!' she cried, racing along the grassy bank.

Further down the track, she

caught sight of a furry grey shape
hunched up against the cold wind.

'Skipper, is that you?' called
Yuma.

Skipper turned round. 'Yuma,
you're all right! Thank goodness! I was
just heading back to get help. I was so
worried about the train—but you must
have stopped it after all?'

'Yes, Kitty stopped
the train,' Pumpkin
said proudly. 'She's
very fast and stronger

than twenty cats!'

'Did you catch the train robbers too?' Skipper demanded. 'Those naughty thieves should be taken straight to the police station.'

Yuma twitched his whiskers awkwardly. 'Please don't be cross, Skipper! But actually, it wasn't a robber that took the train. It was me and Pumpkin.' He explained how they'd accidentally started the engine.

'I know we should

have been more careful, but it really was an accident . . . and we would have stopped the train straight away if the lever hadn't got stuck.' Yuma stared at the ground in embarrassment.

Skipper shook his head. 'Honestly! Haven't I told you millions of times to be careful around engines? Trains and railways are not toys. They are very dangerous things.'

'Sorry, Skipper!' Yuma sniffed and wiped his nose. 'I know it was very silly.'

'I'm sorry too,' said Pumpkin.

'Thank goodness Kitty was here to help.' Skipper turned to Kitty. 'And you figured out how to bring the train back again. How did you work out what to do?'

'Actually, Yuma showed me how to do that,' said Kitty.

Skipper stared at Yuma in amazement. 'You knew how to make the train go backwards?'

'I remembered what you'd shown me,' said Yuma eagerly. 'I'm learning everything I can about trains so I can become a station cat just like you. I think I know a lot already! I can read train timetables and use the station loudspeaker. Best of all, I know how to sound the train whistle!'

'Well, I had no idea!' said Skipper. 'Maybe it would be nice to let

Yuma do more jobs around the station,' Kitty said gently. 'And it would mean you'd get more of a rest.'

'I don't need a rest! Now let's get back to the train.' Skipper limped forwards, holding one paw off the ground. 'Ouch! My poor leg.'

'What happened?' Kitty crouched down to get a better look at Skipper's paw.

'I twisted it when I was jumping down from the lever box,' said Skipper.

Yuma took a bandage out of the

first-aid kit. 'I can bandage it up for you.
I remember the first-aid training you
gave me. Hold this end, Pumpkin.'

Pumpkin held one end of the
bandage while Yuma wrapped it around
Skipper's paw and tied it neatly.

Skipper checked the bandage with a satisfied nod. 'Thanks, Yuma. You've done a good job. Perhaps Kitty is right. There are quite a few jobs you could start doing around the station.'

Yuma gasped. 'Do you mean that? I would love to do more jobs!'

Skipper nodded. 'Yes, it's about time you had more work to do. As long as there are no more mistakes. I'm getting too old to chase runaway trains!'

Yuma's tail waved eagerly. 'I'll be really careful. I promise!'

Kitty gave Skipper a ride on her shoulder and together they walked back to the Red Rocket. They climbed onto the train and then Yuma drove the Red Rocket back to the station, with Skipper giving him careful instructions.

The rain clouds began to clear away, and the stars glittered brightly as they stepped down onto the platform.

Kitty yawned. 'What a wild adventure. I'm glad I got a ride on the Red Rocket, although I'd be happy to sit inside next time and not on the roof!'

Skipper's eyes lit up.
'What a great idea, Kitty!
It's a perfect way for us to
say thank you for saving the
train. You and your family
are welcome to take a ride
tomorrow. I know there are
a few tickets left.'

'That's really kind!' said Kitty.
'But I thought only Very Important
People were allowed to ride on the train
tomorrow.'

'You ARE important, Kitty!'
Skipper rushed into the Station Office
and returned with a bunch of tickets.

Kitty hesitated. 'Are you sure it's all right for me to have them?'

'You should take them,' Pumpkin said firmly. 'You worked hard tonight and just think how excited Max will be.'

'Yes, he'll love it! Thanks, Skipper.' Kitty took four train tickets for her family.

'I suppose we should get back home,' said Pumpkin with a yawn.

'Wait a minute! What about the lost panda?' said Yuma.

'I almost forgot about that,' said Skipper. 'Why don't you check the train? I trust you to do a good job.'

Yuma led Kitty and Pumpkin back onto the Red Rocket and they searched up and down the carriages.

At last Pumpkin found the stuffed panda underneath one of the seats.

'It must have fallen down there,' he said, showing it to Kitty.

'Well done, Pumpkin!' Kitty gave him a hug. 'Let's take the toy back to Minette and Figaro.'

They waved goodbye to the station cats and climbed back to the rooftops. Kitty turned to take one last look at the Red Rocket. Moonlight glinted on its shiny

red carriages and a tiny puff of
steam curled out of the chimney
and vanished quickly in the cold
night air.

Chapter
6

Kitty woke up the next morning
to find Pumpkin, Figaro, and Minette
curled up beside her. Minette was
holding onto Fluff, her lost panda toy,
very tightly as she slept. She'd been
delighted when Kitty brought her toy

back, but she and Figaro had been
too tired to move so they had all
gone to sleep together on Kitty's bed.

Kitty climbed out of bed,
careful not to wake the sleeping cats.
She stuffed the Red Rocket train
tickets up her pyjama sleeve
and hurried downstairs to
look for her parents.

She found Mum making pancakes in the kitchen. Max was sitting at the kitchen table rolling a toy engine up and down.

'Would you like to go back to the station today?' Mum asked her. 'Max is very keen to watch the train set off.'

'Choo-woo!' Max called out, waving his toy engine in the air.

Kitty pulled the train tickets out of her sleeve, grinning. 'I've got an even better idea! How about a ride on the Red Rocket?'

'Goodness, Kitty!' cried Mum.

'Where did you get those?'

Kitty quickly explained about her adventure the night before and the mission to stop the runaway train. 'And Skipper, the station cat, had some spare tickets so he gave them to me to say thank you. I hope it was OK that I took them?'

Mum smiled. 'Yes, of course it was! I'm sure everyone will want to go.'

'I want to go! I want to go!' Max bounced excitedly on his chair.

'I'll tell Dad,' said Mum, quickly dishing up the pancakes, 'And we'd better hurry up and get dressed!'

Kitty ate some pancakes and left some breakfast out for the cats. Ten minutes later, they were all walking down the street to the Hallam City Station.

People were pouring onto the platform, chattering excitedly. The Red Rocket gleamed brightly in the morning sunshine with flower garlands draped over its sides. Gentlemen in smart suits and ladies in elegant, feathered hats were walking down the red carpet and climbing onto the train. Kitty could hardly believe that she was going to ride with all the Very Important People!

Dad lifted Max onto his shoulders. 'Can you see the engine, Max? Doesn't it look fantastic?'

'I wonder how fast it can go,' said Mum.

Kitty smiled. She knew from her adventure last night that the train could go very fast indeed! She looked around, hoping to see Skipper and Yuma.

'All aboard!' called the guard.

'We'd better get on!' said Mum.
'You lead the way, Kitty.'

Tingling with excitement, Kitty
walked down the red carpet and up
the steps onto the train. Mum found
some seats by a window, and they all sat
down together. The engine started to
rumble, and the train whistle sounded.
Max let out a whoop of excitement as
the Red Rocket began to chug slowly
forwards.

Kitty spotted Skipper and Yuma as
they drew out of the station. She waved
at them out of the window and Skipper
waved back with his bandaged paw.

The Red Rocket gained speed and the

cheering crowds disappeared behind
them. Trees and houses flashed past the
window and the train whistle sounded
another cheery choo-woo!

'What a lovely trip,' said Dad.

'I only wish we had some snacks. I forgot
to pack anything.'

'Yes, I'm a bit hungry too,' agreed Mum.

Kitty's eyes lit up. 'I've got an idea.
Let's go to the restaurant carriage and get a
treat from the ice-cream machine!'

Super Facts
About Cats

Super Speed

Have you ever seen a cat make a quick escape from a dog? If so, you'll know that they can move *really* fast—up to 30mph!

Super Hearing

Cats have an incredible sense of hearing and can swivel their large ears to pinpoint even the tiniest of sounds.

Super Reflexes

Have you ever heard the saying 'cats always land on their feet'? People say this because cats have amazing reflexes. If a cat is falling, they can sense quickly how to move their bodies into the right position to land safely.

Super Leaps

A cat can jump over eight feet high
in a single leap; this is due to its powerful
back leg muscles.

Super Vision

Cats have amazing night-time vision. Their
incredible ability to see in low light allows them
to hunt for prey when it's dark outside.

Super Smell

Cats have a very powerful sense of smell,
14 times stronger than a human's. Did you know
that the pattern of ridges on each cat's nose
is as unique as a human's fingerprint?

About the author

Paula Harrison

Before launching a successful writing career,
Paula was a primary school teacher. Her years teaching
taught her what children like in stories and how
they respond to humour and suspense. She went on
to put her experience to good use, writing many
successful stories for young readers.

About the illustrator

Jenny Løvlie

Jenny is a Norwegian illustrator, designer,
creative, foodie, and bird enthusiast. She is fascinated
by the strong bond between humans and animals and
loves using bold colours and shapes in her work.

Love Kitty?
Why not try these too . . .

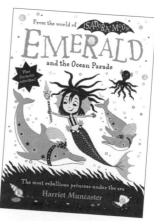